Little Bridge Farm

Socks Cleans Up

...e fête at Little Bridge Farm is going to
... lots of fun. But will Socks be able to
...p clean for the Best Piglet Parade?

Look out for all the Little Bridge Farm books!

Oscar's New Friends

Smudge Finds the Trail

Tiger's Great Adventure

Dilly Saves the Day

Socks Cleans Up

Little Bridge Farm

Socks Cleans Up

PETER CLOVER

Illustrated by Angela Swan

■ SCHOLASTIC

First published in the UK in 2007 by Scholastic Children's Books
An imprint of Scholastic Ltd
Euston House, 24 Eversholt Street
London, NW1 1DB, UK
Registered office: Westfield Road, Southam, Warwickshire, CV47 0RA
SCHOLASTIC and associated logos are trademarks and or registered
trademarks of Scholastic Inc.

Text copyright © Working Partners, 2007
Inside illustrations copyright © Angela Swan, 2007
The rights of Peter Clover and Angela Swan to be identified respectively
as the author and illustrator of this work have been asserted by them.

Cover illustration copyright © Sophy Williams, 2007

10 digit ISBN 1 407 10432 2
13 digit ISBN 978 1407 10432 4

Printed in the UK by CPI Bookmarque, Croydon, CR0 4TD
Papers used by Scholastic Children's Books are made from wood
grown in sustainable forests.

3 5 7 9 10 8 6 4 2

This is a work of fiction. Names, characters, places, incidents and dialogues are
products of the author's imagination or are used fictitiously. Any resemblance
to actual people, living or dead, events or locales is entirely coincidental.

www.scholastic.co.uk/zone

For Vanessa, Robert,
Rebekah and Katrina

Chapter One

Cock-a-doodle-do! Socks the piglet woke up bright and early to the sound of the farmyard cockerel crowing.

What a beautiful morning! he thought, squirming awake with a nice stretch. Socks rolled over in the soft earth, sending clumps of sticky mud flying in all directions. Then his tummy rumbled, reminding him how long ago supper had been. It was definitely time for breakfast!

Socks looked over at Old Spotty. His aunt was still snoring. Socks pushed his head through the wooden rails of the pigsty and pricked up his ears. He could hear his friends waking up noisily, across the yard inside Big Red Barn. But there was no sign of Rosie and Ethan with the morning feed pails.

"W-w-where's our breakfast?" Socks heard Filbert the mountain goat complain loudly. "I'm s-s-starving!"

Socks twirled his corkscrew tail and grinned as Tiger the kitten poked her head through a hole in the barn door.

"Socks!" called Tiger. "Have you seen Rosie and Ethan? Breakfast is late this morning!"

The feed shed door swung open. Farmer Rob's children, Rosie and Ethan, came out swinging bright blue plastic pails in their hands. Rosie's plaits bounced off her shoulders as she skipped along.

"They're coming!" squealed Socks, excitedly. He couldn't wait any longer! Socks looked over his shoulder. Old

Spotty was still sleeping. Socks squirmed and wriggled his plump body through the wooden pigsty rails. It was a tight squeeze, but he sucked in his breath and squeeeeeezed his way through. Then he ran after Rosie and Ethan across the farmyard into Big Red Barn.

Inside the barn, Rosie and Ethan were in a hurry to dish out the breakfast feeds. The stall-gates bounced open and shut behind them as they spilled feed into empty troughs and slopped water into buckets, not stopping to make a fuss of anyone. Socks trotted along behind, huffing and puffing. It was difficult to keep up on his little legs. *Why are they so late?* thought Socks. His tummy rumbled loudly as he followed the two children around the barn, trying to get himself noticed. *I wonder what's going on.*

"W-w-what? Only one c-c-carrot this morning!" grumbled Filbert, staring into his pail. His long, straggly hair swept the

floor as he hoovered up spilled pellets off the floor. The greedy goat snaffled one of Oscar's apples as the young pony arched his neck, waiting for his morning pat. But after filling his trough, Rosie and Ethan walked right past.

Parsley, the Jack Russell terrier, rolled on to her back and waggled her legs in the air. But even Parsley didn't get her pink tummy tickled as she usually did. And even when Tiger the kitten mewed really loudly and brushed up against Rosie's leg, Rosie took no notice at all.

Socks's tummy grumbled again as the animals gobbled their breakfasts. Rosie and Ethan were in such a hurry this morning. Socks suddenly realized that they'd accidentally skipped *his* breakfast.

"Hey! What about me?" oinked Socks as he followed the two children outside. "I'm starving!"

Rosie and Ethan ignored Socks, threw down their empty feed pails, and ran towards the main gates at White Stone Bridge.

Socks poked his head back into the barn. "There must be something going on," he said to his friends. "Let's go and find out what!"

Socks and all his farmyard friends hurried out of the barn and along to the bridge. Farmer Rob was at the gates, fixing a big banner across the entrance to Little Bridge Farm. The animals watched as the children helped tie the ends in place.

The banner had colourful writing painted across it.

"I wonder what it says," whickered Oscar.

Socks couldn't read, either. But he had seen a banner just like this before.

"I know! I know what it is," Socks squealed. "I've seen Farmer Rob put up a banner just like this one before," he explained to the other animals. "It means that there's going to be a fête at Little Bridge Farm."

Tiger screwed up her nose and looked at Socks.

"What's a fête?" she asked.

"It's like a big party," said Socks. "I was only little at the time, but I remember all the people from the village coming along to the farm and bringing their animals. There are games, and competitions, and prizes, and—"

"F-F-FOOD," interrupted Filbert. "I remember now. There are tables everywhere piled high with lots of lovely f-f-food. It's soooooo exciting!"

"That's right," remembered Parsley. "They have a big picnic like you've never seen before."

Smudge the Labrador puppy licked his lips.

"And all the animals get to eat the leftovers. Do you remember Lucy's wonderful apple pie?" said Socks.

"Mmmmm. That was the best bit of all." Filbert rolled his eyes and Socks saw Filbert's legs wobble as the goat almost fainted at the memory. Lucy, Ethan and Rosie's mum, baked the best apple pies in the world.

Socks's tummy rumbled again. He still hadn't had any breakfast!

Now they could see Ethan and Rosie tying brightly coloured ribbons around the gate posts.

"I wonder who Farmer Rob will be entering into the competitions this year," said Parsley. The animals looked round at each other.

"At the last fête," Socks said, "There were prizes for all kinds of things. Sheep herding for the big dogs. Hunt-and-find for the puppies. A cute chick contest. A prettiest kitten award. There was even a special prize for the best animal in the whole show."

"Oh, I hope I d-d-don't win that!" said Filbert. "I'd never be able to climb up on to the winner's podium. I d-d-don't like heights!"

"You'd be too busy pinching food to enter any competitions," said Socks, laughing.

The animals wandered back to the farmyard. Socks twirled his tail as he remembered the Piglet Parade.

I wonder which piglet will be entered this year? he thought. *I bet it feels great to lead the parade!* He splashed through a muddy puddle. Socks loved mud. It might be messy, but it felt so good. There was no way he'd ever be able to stay on his best

9

behaviour, all clean and tidy, for a piglet parade. *It won't be me leading the parade, that's for sure*, Socks said to himself, as he looked down at his muddy trotters. But he couldn't help wondering who would be good enough to enter the contest. He would just have to wait and find out.

Chapter Two

Socks, Smudge and Clarissa the chick followed Rosie and Ethan around the farmyard as the children prepared for the afternoon's fête.

The animals watched as Rosie and Ethan carried tables out of the store shed and set them up in the lower field. Farmer Rob was already there, putting up a big marquee tent with his eldest son, Jack.

"What are they doing over there?" asked Smudge, trotting into the middle of the field for a closer look. Farm

workers were laying down hay bales in a
big circle.

"Looks like a show ring," said Socks,
snuffling his snout into the golden bales,
"for all the contests and competitions."

Smudge trotted over to Rosie to
investigate, and she chuckled as the
puppy weaved himself in and out of her
legs. Clarissa strutted her way into the
middle of the show ring, puffed out her
feathers, and shook her tiny wings.

"I'm going to be the star of the show,"
she clucked.

"What about a game of tag instead?"
Socks squealed. "Coming to get you!" he
laughed as he chased after the cheeky
chicken. Socks and Smudge tumbled and
tripped over each other as they chased a
squawking Clarissa out of the ring.

Clarissa fluttered up into the branches
of a tree.

Socks got his breath back then puffed

out his chest. *I think I might do a bit of parading of my own!* He stuck his muddy snout in the air and marched round the ring, lifting his little trotters high in the air. He imagined what it would feel like hearing everyone clapping and calling his name. *Socks! Socks! Socks!* He could almost hear the crowds cheering.

"Hey!" called Smudge as he joined Socks in the ring. "Looks like you're dreaming about the contests."

"No, I'm not," said Socks, feeling embarrassed and stopping dead in his tracks. "I'm not doing anything."

"Yes you are!" teased Smudge. "I bet you'd really like to be entered in the Piglet Parade, wouldn't you?"

"I don't think so," said Socks. "I'd much rather be free all day to enjoy myself at the fête! Being on best behaviour all day for a competition doesn't sound like much fun to me." Socks gave a snort. He struggled with good behaviour at the best of times. "Besides," he added. "Keeping clean and tidy all day would be double difficult and really boring!"

Socks, Smudge and Clarissa (who had come down from the tree) made their way back to the barn. They saw Daisy and Duke, the two giant shire horses, standing in the doorway of the barn with all the grown-up animals. The grown-ups were huddled together in a group.

"They look as if they're having a meeting about something," said Socks.

Socks, Smudge and Clarissa slowed down, then stumbled to a halt, as the grown-ups turned to look at them.

"What's going on?" asked Socks as Trumpet came bounding over. The big sheepdog licked the top of Smudge's head.

"We should start practising your sniffing skills, Smudge," said the Old English sheepdog. "I've just heard that Farmer Rob has entered you for the puppies' hunt-and-find contest!"

"Hooray!" yapped Smudge. "Can we start now?" He pushed his nose at the earth and started sniffing in circles.

"You should practise in the woods," advised Trumpet. "There are some great scents to follow there."

Smudge pricked up his ears at that idea.

"But I'd better come with you," added Trumpet. "There was a fox sniffing around the woods yesterday. I don't want you to practise there on your own."

"See you later, Socks," called Smudge as he rushed away with Trumpet.

Socks stomped in a puddle and splashed Clarissa as her mum flapped her wings and strutted over.

"Come along, little C," clucked the big,

red hen. "Back to the hen house to practise your strutting and clucking."

"Why?" asked Clarissa shaking her feathers.

"I want you to impress the judges in the Cute Chick contest," her mum said, proudly. "You've been entered as the Little Bridge Farm contestant."

"See you at the fête, Socks," chirped Clarissa excitedly, as she followed her mum back to the coop.

Socks watched Clarissa leave.

"Good luck!" he called after her.

Poor things, thought Socks. *Fancy having to practise for competitions on a lovely day like today.* Socks wandered into the farmyard and scratched his dirty neck on a fence post.

Lucky me! I've got the whole day to do whatever I like! Socks thought about it. There was so much fun to have on such a sunny morning! So many muddy puddles to roll in.

"I can, I can. . ." Socks's voice faded to nothing, as he suddenly realized he was talking to himself. No one was around. All of his friends had gone off to practise. Socks was on his own.

Chapter Three

"Ahem!" Someone behind Socks cleared their throat. Socks glanced back over his shoulder and saw Old Spotty looking right at him.

The old sow was taking a bath in a pool of mud. She fixed Socks with her eyes and flapped an ear at him. Socks knew exactly what that meant. He trotted over to see what his aunt wanted. NO ONE disobeyed Old Spotty.

Socks was about to do a brilliant belly-flop into Old Spotty's mud bath when the old sow raised a warning trotter.

"Stop!" she bellowed.

Socks froze on the spot. His corkscrew tail quivered. Socks had no idea what he had done wrong!

"You can't wallow in the mud today," said Old Spotty.

"Uhh!" Socks grunted and went to sit down.

"Stop!" oinked Old Spotty again. "Don't sit. It's dirty!"

Socks looked behind him at the ground. He had no idea what his aunt was talking about; he was *always* dirty! The soft earth seemed a perfectly normal place to sit. All nice and squidgy. And he was already muddy from his romps this morning.

"Over there!" ordered Old Spotty. "Go and stand over there on that clean, flat stone." The other piglets had been listening and giggled at Socks's confusion.

He stood, shuffling his feet on the

stone. "It's not very comfortable," complained Socks quietly. Old Spotty took no notice.

"From now on," she explained, "there will be no wallowing in mud, no sitting on earth, no snouting around in the dirt. AND NO MESSY FOOD." She sounded really serious.

"What?" Socks's jaw dropped open. The other piglets laughed even louder at Socks's puzzled face. "Have I done something wrong?" Old Spotty shook her head and huffed a big sigh.

"The fête," she told Socks. "You've

been entered in the best Piglet Parade. And that means you have to stay as clean and tidy as possible between now and this afternoon."

The Best Piglet Parade! Socks couldn't believe what he was hearing. *Oh, no! I've been entered in a contest!*

"And I'm determined," announced Old Spotty, "that YOU are going to win first prize and lead this year's Piglet Parade around Little Bridge Farm."

Socks was surprised that he had been chosen to represent the piglets at the fête. Everyone knew how much Socks liked to get messed up. Young piglets were born to roll in the mud! Besides . . . Socks wasn't even sure that he *wanted* to be in the competition. Not when it meant being as good as gold – all day!

"No mud?" Socks asked .

"Not another drop!" Old Spotty confirmed.

The other piglets didn't help at all. They all teased their older cousin by joining Old Spotty and jumping in the muddy bath.

"Oooohhh! This cool mud feels sooo nice," squealed Patch, the youngest piglet. Patch had a big, brown splodge across his back and always looked like he was covered in mud.

"Especially now that the day is heating up!" Snow grinned. She squirmed on to her back and waggled her little snow-white trotters in the air. "Lovely, lovely, cooooool mud," she teased.

"Aren't you coming in, Socks?" giggled Pudge, the fattest piglet of the

bunch. "Or are you going to have to stay clean and pink all day long?"

Old Spotty gave the three piglets an icy glare. Then she looked back at Socks.

"Don't take any notice of these three," she grunted. "All that matters is that you win this contest. I heard Rosie say that she will be coming along shortly to get you ready, and give you a bubble bath!"

"A BUBBLE BATH!" spluttered the other piglets. "You won't even look like a pig!"

Socks held his snout high in the air and tried to ignore his cousins' giggles and taunts. He didn't like being laughed at.

Being clean isn't so bad, he thought. He only hoped that he could make Old Spotty proud. Winning the contest seemed so important to her. *They won't be laughing when I lead the Piglet Parade around Little Bridge Farm.*

Socks was suddenly determined to try his hardest.

I'll show everyone! I'll be the cleanest pig there ever was!

Chapter Four

Rosie walked into the pigsty carefully carrying a small, plastic bath filled with hot water. Socks watched as Rosie topped up the tub with the hosepipe and added a few drops of bubble bath.

"Oooooohh! What a lovely, clean, soapy, smell," teased Patch. "You're going to smell like a beautiful flower, Socks."

Socks turned his head and took no notice. He sniffed the water. The bubble bath *did* smell good.

Rosie sat down on an upturned milk pail.

"Come on, boy. You're going to be our prize piglet," said Rosie, as she lifted Socks and popped him into the soapy tub.

The bath water was lovely and warm against his skin. Socks blew soapy suds off the end of his snout as Rosie began to sponge him down. The rough sponge tickled his back. Warm, soapy suds settled on his head.

"Don't forget to wash behind his ears," taunted Patch, Snow and Porky, as they crept forward for a better look.

Socks looked at his cousins. They seemed a little jealous of all the attention Socks was getting. And secretly, Socks was quite enjoying the bath – although he would never admit it to any of the others!

"You look beautiful," Rosie said, drying him off with a big, fluffy towel. "And you smell gorgeous! You're bound to win first prize." She tied a big yellow ribbon around his neck and clapped her hands together in delight. Socks had never been so squeaky clean in his life.

This is a little embarrassing! Socks thought. He was sure he looked silly in the bow. *I just hope none of the other animals see me wearing this, before the contest.*

"You look wonderful," said Old Spotty, oinking proudly. "Now you must

28

stay just like that so you can win the contest."

He watched Rosie skip happily away back to the farmhouse. Old Spotty headed back to her mud bath.

They both seem so pleased, thought Socks. *I'll wear the bow for Rosie, and for Old Spotty.* He only hoped that he wouldn't disappoint them.

Socks needed a stay-clean plan. After a moment, he knew just what to do. He could wait in the quiet, mud-free barn – and hopefully none of his friends would see him in his bow! The other animals were all out in the fields and wood, practising for their own competitions in the fête.

Socks picked his way carefully across the farmyard towards the barn, lifting his little trotters high to avoid any dirty puddles. It was very tempting to roll in the mud, but Socks had promised himself he wouldn't. He knew how much winning this contest would mean to Rosie and Old Spotty.

"It's amazing how easy it is to get messed up," Socks said to himself, "when you're trying to stay clean and tidy!"

He hadn't gone far when he noticed that someone had spilled a pool of milk outside the cow sheds.

"My," purred Cider the farm cat, looking up at Socks as she lapped at the milk. "Don't you look the cat's whiskers?" Socks gave an embarrassed smile as he stepped neatly over the creamy puddle and hurried away.

Up ahead, the wheels of Farmer Rob's tractor had churned a long track of squidgy mud which spread right across the yard. He was very tempted, for a moment, to forget the contest and dive in. But he didn't. Not today. It was a BIG challenge for him to try and stay clean and tidy. And he was determined to give it his best shot.

Several clods of grass sat in clumps amongst the mud, making a path to Big Red Barn.

"I can balance on those clods," said Socks. "And use them as stepping stones. Easy peasy!"

He placed one front trotter carefully on the first clump of grass. Socks felt it slide a little beneath his foot. *Careful!* he thought. Then he reached to put another trotter on the next clod of grass. His little plump body was stretched out, right across the mud. Socks looked down. His bow dangled dangerously near the mud. Two worms wriggled just beneath his belly. Suddenly, Socks felt his back legs slipping away behind him.

Oh, no! This isn't as easy as I thought! There was nothing for it. Socks took a chance and jumped forward, landing almost clear of the muddy track. His back legs splashed in the muddy water.

"Phew! That was almost a disaster!" he

said. Socks looked down at himself. "Not bad. Only a few specks of dirt!"

Socks poked his head through the door of Big Red Barn. He was in luck. All the stalls were empty. All except one.

Filbert was still in his stall. "N-n-n-nice bow, Socks."

Socks felt his cheeks flush red. "Where is everyone?"

"Practising, I think," mumbled Filbert, as he snuffled around the stalls looking for titbits.

Suddenly Filbert stopped snuffling. He lifted his nose in the air and sniffed.

"What is it?" Socks started to ask. Then he twitched his own snout. His nostrils suddenly smelt the most delicious, yummy smell wafting past his nose from outside. The smell was so wonderful and fruity that Socks knew what it was straight away. His mouth watered at the thought.

Socks looked at Filbert.

32

Filbert looked at Socks.

"You know what it is, don't you?" Socks asked the straggly goat. "It's one of Lucy's famous apple pies!"

"Last one to the farmhouse goes hungry!" Filbert challenged, and ran out of the barn as fast as he could. Socks suddenly remembered – he still hadn't had any breakfast! He turned round and chased after Filbert.

"Wait for me!" he cried out. "And please let one of the pies be burnt," he muttered to himself. All the animals knew that if an apple pie was burnt, the farmer's wife would throw it out and give it to the animals. Socks could almost taste the sweet apple filling and the crispy, crunchy pastry.

As he ran, he noticed a second smell. A slightly toasty one. It was the smell of burnt pastry. "Yippee!" Socks cried, as he turned the corner of the farmhouse. Then he skidded to a halt. Filbert, Clarissa,

Oscar, Cider, Parsley and a crowd of Socks's friends were already waiting patiently in line outside the kitchen door.

Socks looked down at his big yellow

bow. Everyone he was trying to avoid was here! But no one seemed to take any notice of how he was looking, and apple pie was worth the embarrassment!

"Oh, I sooo love apple p-p-pie," Filbert stammered, skittering excitedly. Duke was next in the queue.

"Get in line, Socks," said the big shire horse. "And wait patiently. Everyone wants a piece of Lucy's pie."

Socks went to sit down, but suddenly remembered to keep his bum clean and jumped up again.

Then the door opened and Lucy came out holding the burnt apple pie. She smiled when she saw the crowd of animals waiting outside. "I suppose you're all glad I've burnt one of my pies!" she said.

Socks licked his snout. He could almost taste the apples beneath the toasty pie crust.

Socks pushed forward as Lucy scooped the ruined pie into the scraps trough. The pastry burst open and the sweet apple filling spilled out.

All the animals rushed forward. Socks suddenly forgot all about staying clean as he pushed and squirmed his way to the front of the crowd with the others. The pie smelled so good.

"Apple pie, here I come!" Socks called out in delight. But just as he was about to take a big bite, he felt something pull him up by the scruff of his neck. His trotters lifted off the cobbles and suddenly Socks was flying through the air!

Chapter Five

"Let me down!" Socks squealed.

Duke lowered his head and put Socks gently back down on the ground, away from the feed trough.

Socks looked up at the giant horse. He couldn't understand why Duke had done that. Didn't he want Socks to enjoy the apple pie?

"Sorry," Duke said. "Old Spotty's orders. No messy food. No crumbly pastry. And definitely no sticky apple filling!"

Socks shook his head in disbelief.

"Can't I just have one small piece of Lucy's apple pie? Just one tiny piece?"

But while he watched, all the pie was gobbled up. Filbert was already licking the empty trough clean.

"This is really g-g-good," stammered Filbert with his mouth full of crumbs.

"I'm sorry," Duke said. "Old Spotty's orders. But there's dry food pellets in the other trough, over there. If you're hungry, you can eat those."

"*If* I'm hungry?" Socks said, getting to his feet. "I'm starving!"

Socks wanted to make Old Spotty proud, but missing out on apple pie was the worst! He looked down at his yellow ribbon and let out a big sigh.

"This Piglet Parade had better be worth it," he grumbled, as he wandered over to eat some dry food pellets.

The hot sun had risen high in the sky. It was just the day for a nice, cooling mud bath. But not for Socks. Suddenly, Smudge came bounding up, wagging his tail.

"I've just finished hunt-and-find practice in the woods," woofed Smudge. "It was brilliant! I'm going to play with Monty in Pebble Pond now. Do you want to come along?"

Socks glanced at the neat satin ribbon, tied into a big yellow bow at his neck, and then shook his head. "I can't get wet," he said, sighing. "Old Spotty would never forgive me."

"You do look sweet," teased Smudge.

"But what harm would there be, if you come along and just watch from the shade of a tree?"

"It would be lovely and cool by the pond," Socks agreed. "OK. I'll just make sure I stay well away from the water." He followed Smudge along to Pebble Pond.

When they got there, Monty the moorhen was already jumping in and out of the shallow water from the bank. *Splash! Splash! Splash!* He was having great fun all on his own.

"Don't splash me!" cried Socks. "I mustn't get wet." Socks couldn't believe he'd just said that as he hurried to stand in the shade of a tree away from the water. *This contest is spoiling all my fun,* thought Socks.

"Let's play a game," suggested Monty. "Let's pick stones up off the pond bed and see who can collect the most!"

Socks tried not to be too jealous of his

friends as they took it in turns to hold their breath and duck their heads below the water. This was one of his favourite games. Socks would have given anything to dip his head in the cool pond water. The day was getting hotter and hotter by the minute. But Socks was determined to stay clean and dry.

Monty and Smudge were having lots of fun lining up rows of pebbles on the bank.

"That's five to me," said Monty, dropping another shiny pebble from his beak on to the grass.

"And five to me," said Smudge, shaking the water from his ears. They both had five pebbles each.

Suddenly, Monty stretched his neck and peered deeper into the water. "Wow! Just look at that one," he whistled. "There's a pebble way down there with a streak of silver running through it."

Smudge stuck his head under the

water. "You should see this, Socks," he spluttered. "It's fantastic!"

"Whoever gets that pebble," suggested Socks, "should win the game!" Socks couldn't join in, but at least he could help with the rules. Socks imagined the silver streaked pebble glinting below the surface of the water as Monty and Smudge took it in turns to duck and dive.

Smudge gave an enormous sneeze and blew water from his nostrils. "Nearly got it that time!"

"I'm bound to win," whistled Monty, ducking beneath the surface for the umpteenth time.

Socks couldn't resist the urge to creep closer to the water's edge, hoping to catch a glimpse of the silver pebble.

"I know the best way to get it!" Smudge shouted.

Socks gasped as Smudge launched himself off the bank, and made a huge splash as he hit the water.

"Watch out!" squealed Socks. But it was too late. Socks cried out in shock as the pond water splashed all over him.

When Smudge surfaced, he held the silver pebble firmly in his soft mouth. Socks stood on the bank with water dripping from his ears and snout. Smudge had soaked Socks from head to trotter.

Socks looked down at himself and saw the yellow ribbon hanging limply from his neck. *Oh no!* Socks thought. *I'm drenched.*

"Sorry," said Smudge. "Got a bit carried away!" He climbed out of the pond and trotted over to Socks.

"A spot of water never hurt anyone," whistled Monty. But Socks wasn't so sure. There was pond weed in the water and it was drying in green patches on his clean, pink skin.

"Just look at my bow," squealed Socks.

"It isn't a bow any more," said Smudge.

"I know," said Socks. "Now it's just a wrinkly old piece of ribbon." His pink skin was turning a funny shade of green. Socks looked back up at his friends. "I hope Old Spotty doesn't notice anything!"

Chapter Six

Socks trotted across the courtyard and tried to slip quietly into the pigsty without Old Spotty seeing him.

The old sow was dozing in her usual mud bath. But Old Spotty never missed a trick. As Socks tiptoed past, she opened one sharp eye.

Socks tried to duck into the covered shelter.

"Socks!" boomed Old Spotty. Socks froze on the spot.

"Come back here at once!" she ordered.

Old Spotty sat up with a big, squelching sound as wet mud dripped from her belly and jowls. She stared hard at Socks.

"What on earth have you done?" she bellowed. "Look at your ribbon. And your skin! It's all green!"

Socks shrunk back and wished that he could disappear completely. He had never heard his aunt sound so angry.

"It's not *that* bad, is it?" he asked.

"It's worse than BAD!" snorted Old Spotty. "What did I tell you about how important it was to stay clean and tidy for the parade?"

"Don't worry!" oinked Socks, feeling terrible for disappointing Old Spotty. "Perhaps Rosie can tidy me up again. I'll go and see her."

"You'd better!" said Old Spotty, crossly.

Socks trotted across the yard towards the cottage. He found Rosie sitting on the swing seat, on the covered porch. Socks was expecting Rosie to be really cross, but Rosie only laughed.

"Oh, you mucky little piglet!" Rosie smiled. "What have you been up to? Stay there, Socks," she said. "I'll be back in two shakes." Rosie ducked into the cottage.

From up on the porch, Socks could see people wandering around the farmyard. Cars had started to arrive outside the main gates. And lots of people were already crossing White Stone Bridge. The fête would start soon.

Rosie came back with a bowl of soapy water and a sponge. She sponged Socks's skin squeaky clean. Then she tied a bright purple ribbon around his neck.

"Look at you now, Socks," Rosie said, smiling. "You look even better than you did before!"

Socks squealed with excitement and puffed out his little pink chest. He wasn't going to let Old Spotty down, after all. Socks suddenly felt in a much better mood. Luckily, there wasn't much time left to get messed up again. The fête was about to start. All Socks had to do was to stay clean and tidy for a teeny bit longer and wait for the Piglet Parade. Easy!

Little Bridge Farm was buzzing with people. Parsley came scooting up to Socks, yapping excitedly. The energetic dog could hardly catch her breath.

"The fête's started," she babbled.

"Come on, Socks! Let's go."

The two friends hurried down to the lower field to have a quick look round and check out the stalls and animal pens.

"I wonder if Pinkie will be there," said Socks.

"Who's Pinkie?" asked Parsley.

"Don't you remember?" oinked Socks. "Pinkie won the Perfect Piglet contest at the last fête. She's beautiful."

A village band had been set up in the corner of the field, and the musicians were already playing. Children held hands and were dancing in a big circle around the bandstand. Parents and other grown-ups were busy laying out food and fizzy drinks on the wooden tables.

The two friends walked across to the holding pens to say hello to the visiting animals. A special area had been set up and marked out in rows with ropes and wooden posts.

Socks and Parsley peered through the pens and rubbed welcome noses with all the visitors. There were sheep, ponies, goats, dogs, horses, chickens, geese and of course . . . pigs.

Socks poked his snout between the wooden slats of the pig pens to say hello. He spotted a perfect piglet.

"Hello, Pinkie," oinked Socks, cheerfully. "I'm Socks."

"Hi, Socks," replied Pinkie. Her rosy pink skin was g l o w i n g and spotless. She fluttered her long white lashes at Socks. Socks felt his face blush bright red. To hide his embarrassment, he looked round the stall. All the piglets were getting on really well, chatting and squealing together. But suddenly, one by one, they all fell silent.

"What is it?" asked Socks. "What's wrong?"

"We've just seen the biggest sow ever!" gasped Pinkie. "She's absolutely enormous. And watch out, she's coming this way!"

"That'll be my aunt," Socks said, proudly. But when he turned around to introduce Old Spotty to his new friends, he could see that the big sow was far from happy. Her brows were creased into a deep frown. And she was flapping her ears. Not a good sign!

"Socks," she bellowed. "What do you think you are you doing? You shouldn't be talking with the rival competitors."

All the other piglets quickly scurried to the back of the holding pens. "You'll never win this contest," added Old Spotty, "if you get friendly with the other piglets. You just won't have the right attitude!" She shook her head with disappointment and nudged Socks with her snout, away from the pens, towards the show ring.

"Go and stand over there," she said, firmly. "Wait for the Perfect Piglet contest to be called. Then go out and try to WIN!"

Socks lowered his head and did as he was told.

But what if I don't win? he thought. *What if I don't even come close?* Socks didn't really care much about winning for himself. But he really didn't want to let down Old Spotty.

Chapter Seven

Socks stood at the edge of the show ring, waiting for the Piglet Parade entries to be called.

Not long now, thought Socks. *All I've got to do is stay clean for just a few more moments.*

The piglet's contest was the second competition on the fête's programme. Farmer Rob marched into the ring and rang a hand bell. This was the signal to let everyone know that the contests were about to begin. The band played a short fanfare as the farmer announced the first contest: the Best Baby Bunny Competition.

Socks twirled his tail as Rosie walked into the ring, carefully nursing a basket full of tiny baby bunnies.

As the crowd gathered round to watch, Smudge bounded into the ring. The little puppy was so excited that he bounced in front of Rosie. Poor Rosie stumbled and almost tripped. She sat down on the grass with a thump. The lid of the basket flipped open. And before anyone could do anything, five fluffy bunnies had escaped!

"Oh, no," cried Rosie, as all the bunnies hopped off in different directions.

Rosie scrambled to her feet and chased
after them.

"Poor Rosie," said Socks. "And
those silly bunnies would be
easier to catch if they stood
still!"

Socks watched as other
children and grown ups ran
around trying to help. One by one they
caught the baby rabbits and popped
them back into the basket. But only Socks
noticed that one naughty bunny had
hopped out again. The fluffy little rabbit
looked around quickly, then flattened its
ears and bounded straight out of the
show ring, towards the apple orchard.

Socks squealed loudly, but Rosie didn't take any notice. She was busy smoothing down her dress after the tumble. Socks stomped his little trotters in the grass, trying to get someone's attention.

"Why won't anyone listen to me?" he oinked. But nobody took any notice of Socks as the contestants lined up for the start of the bunny contest.

Socks didn't waste another second. That little bunny was only a tiny baby; anything could happen to her! Without stopping to think about anything else, Socks chased after the escaped rabbit. He thought he heard Old Spotty calling after him but Socks didn't stop. The bunny was in danger. Her white cotton-wool tail was bobbing up and down in the distance. The bunny had almost reached the orchard.

Socks ran faster. The apple orchard was very close to the woods. And Socks remembered what Trumpet had told

Smudge earlier: a fox had been seen on the prowl!

With another flash of her white bobtail

the bunny disappeared into the shady ferns which grew beneath the fruit trees in the orchard.

Socks plunged into the undergrowth

and charged through the ferns looking for the bunny. His beautiful purple ribbon soon got caught on the sharp prickles of a thorn bush. It ripped into shreds.

Socks looked around. He glanced one way – then another. Suddenly, Socks saw a flash of white cottontail as the bunny hopped from behind a tree stump and stopped up ahead to nibble some dandelion leaves. Between Socks and the bunny were mushy apples that had fallen to the ground.

Out of the corner of his eye Socks suddenly saw a flash of orange fur poking out from underneath a nearby bush. "Oh, no!" he cried. "The fox!"

The fox crept farther out of the bushes as it sniffed the bunny's scent. Socks felt his heart thumping. He had to act quickly. Nothing else mattered. He had to get across that patch of mushy apples – fast! The bunny was only a few hops away from the bush. And the crafty fox was lying in wait. There was only one thing to do. Socks took a deep breath . . . and charged.

Chapter Eight

Socks ran as fast as his little trotters would carry him towards the bunny. The fox leapt out of the bush. Socks had never been this close to a fox before. He could see the long white whiskers stretching out from its twitching nose. The fox's orange fur glistened as it crept closer to the bunny. Socks could see that the fox had plans – and they weren't very nice plans.

Socks stumbled and slipped on the patch of the mushy apples. Squashed apples stuck to his body as he rolled

over on the ground and slid across the
messy pulp.

Socks skidded right between the fox
and the bunny, bowling the fox over
backwards.

Socks let out a really loud squeal. The
fox was so surprised and frightened that
it ran off. The baby rabbit was shaking
with fright. After all, she'd had quite a
shock. She looked up at Socks and
trembled.

"Don't be scared, little bunny,"

said Socks, soothingly. "That nasty fox has gone. You're safe now with me."

Socks looked down at himself. He was covered in apple mush, leaves and dry ferns. He must look like a scary green monster. His ribbon was in tatters. Oh no! He was never going to win the Piglet Parade now. But Socks had saved the tiny bunny.

The bunny whimpered softly. "I want my mummy!"

"Then we had better take you home," said Socks.

Socks couldn't decide what he felt as he trotted home with the little bunny hopping alongside. He knew he'd ruined his chances in the Piglet Parade. But he felt proud as he brought the rabbit safely back into the field.

Trumpet came bounding over. "What's happened?" he asked.

All Socks's friends crowded round to listen.

"Socks saved me from a nasty fox," said the bunny, in a tiny, squeaky voice. "It was hiding in the orchard!" She trembled at the memory. Socks nuzzled her ears with his snout.

Socks could tell that Trumpet and everyone were impressed. A small crowd of humans and other animals had gathered at the field gate. When they saw Socks they stared hard with their mouths hanging open.

"Wow, Socks! You're so cool!" said his young cousin, Patch.

"You're brilliant," said Snow.

"A real hero!" agreed Porky.

Socks held his head high. "Thanks," he said.

"It's not every day that a piglet scares a fox and saves a bunny!" said Trumpet.

But just then Old Spotty pushed her way to the front of the crowd. "Look at the state of you!" she shouted.

Socks glanced down at himself again.

He was still covered from head to trotter in a mushy apple mess of autumn leaves and ferns. Socks looked back at Old Spotty as his aunt shook her head slowly from side to side.

"I can't believe what you've done, Socks!" said the old sow. "After everything I told you, you just ran off and got yourself all messed up. Didn't you care anything at all about the contest?"

"Y-y-yes!!" stammered Socks. "I tried really hard to stay clean. But then the bunny. . ."

"Yes, isn't he fantastic?" interrupted Trumpet. "Saving that bunny all by himself. You must be very proud of him, Old Spotty."

"Bunny! What bunny?" Old Spotty seemed to be the only one who didn't know what Socks had *really* done. She had been so busy thinking about the Piglet Parade.

Trumpet explained about the daring rescue.

"Ahem!" grunted the sow as she realized what a hero Socks had been. Her face softened and, for a moment, she seemed lost for words. "You saved the little bunny all by yourself?"

"I'm sorry I let you down!" oinked Socks, desperately. "I did try to stay clean. I guess I'm just a messy piglet and not really cut out for competitions!"

"I'm the one who's sorry," said Old Spotty. "I can see how silly I've been. There are other things far more important than staying clean and winning a silly contest!"

Old Spotty gave Socks a loving nudge. "And anyway," she added. "You look more like my Socks when you're covered in mud!"

All the other animals gathered around in a circle.

"I b-b-bet you could easily win a

messy p-p-piglet prize," stammered
Filbert.

Old Spotty gave Filbert an icy glare.
"S-s-sorry. Only j-j-joking!"

"But it's not too late," wooffed Parsley.
"We could easily clean up Socks and
have him looking as good as new in no
time!"

Chapter Nine

Soon Monty was tying the best bow he'd ever tied from a piece of blue seed-sack – even though it did look like a rather scruffy bird's nest hanging from Socks's neck.

"There you go!" whistled Monty. "Best bow, ever!"

But without Rosie's bubble bath it was difficult to get Socks looking perfect.

"You look really l-l-lovely," mumbled Filbert. Socks wasn't so sure.

Farmer Rob rang the hand bell and

announced the start of the Perfect Piglet Parade. Socks ran over, just in the nick of time. He puffed hard, trying to catch his breath as Old Spotty nudged him proudly into the show ring.

"It doesn't matter what you look like," she grunted softly in his ear. "You're already OUR winner."

Socks held his head high, twirled his tail and trotted into the ring. He stood in line behind Pinkie.

"You were very brave, chasing that fox away and saving the bunny," Pinkie said. "You're a real hero!" All the other

piglets in the competition agreed.

The judges walked up and down the line, examining the contestants. Compared to all the others, Socks did look a bit scruffy. But he didn't care. All his friends were there watching. And Old Spotty looked so proud of him.

The judges spoke with Farmer Rob. The farmer grinned and made an announcement.

"This year," he began. "The winner of the Best Piglet contest is. . ." A hushed silence fell across the crowd. "For the second year running, Pinkie."

The crowd broke into a round of applause. Socks huffed a sigh as he looked across at all his friends. He was happy for Pinkie, but secretly, he felt a little disappointed all the same. Even though he didn't really think he had a chance of winning.

"HOWEVER!" announced Farmer Rob in a booming voice that made everyone sit up. "This year, there is an additional contest . . . and the winner of this *special* contest . . . will lead the Piglet Parade."

The crowd fell silent again.

"I wonder what it is?" whispered Socks.

"Please put your hands together," announced Farmer Rob, "for the winner of this year's special contest – the Messiest Piglet Prize."

Everyone listened. Socks held his breath.

"The winner is . . . Socks!"

Socks almost jumped out of his skin.

All his friends clapped and cheered so loudly that the birds flew out of the tree on Great Oak Hill. Socks's friends couldn't cheer or whoop enough. Monty whistled, the dogs barked, the chickens clucked, the pigs squealed and the horses neighed.

Socks took his place in the centre of the show ring. Rosie was laughing and clapping her hands excitedly.

"This year's Piglet Parade," continued Farmer Rob, "will be led by Socks from Little Bridge Farm."

Socks swallowed a lump in his throat. He blinked back the tears in his eyes. He had never felt so proud.

"Well done," oinked Pinkie. "Everyone wanted you to lead the parade."

"You're the best piglet," said Shadow.

Farmer Rob pinned the winner's red rosette to Socks's ribbon. Socks led the parade of piglets and other animals around the farm.

"Three cheers for Socks," called Trumpet, as the parade headed back to Big Red Barn.

"Hip, hip, hoorah!" everyone cheered. Socks felt fantastic.

"I think we've all learnt a very important lesson today," said Old Spotty, wisely. "There are more important things in life to think about than what you look like! Now, close your eyes for a moment, Socks."

All the animals giggled as Socks did as he was told.

"OPEN!" cried all the animals, together, as Filbert produced a big piece of Lucy's apple pie from behind one of the stalls.

"We've been s-s-saving this for you," stammered Filbert. The greedy goat licked his lips with a naughty glint in his eye.

"FILBERT!" boomed Old Spotty. "Don't you dare eat one single crumb!"

Socks tucked into the best treat ever. He hadn't done a very good job of staying clean and tidy, but it didn't seem to matter any more. Socks was a hero! But more important than that, Old Spotty still loved him. No matter how messy he was.

"Thanks everyone," he said, talking through a mouth full of pie. "This is the very best end to a perfect day!"